Dear Parents and Educators,

Welcome to Penguin Young Readers! As parents and educators, you know that each child develops at his or her own pace—in terms of speech, critical thinking, and, of course, reading. Penguin Young Readers recognizes this fact. As a result, each Penguin Young Readers book is assigned a traditional easy-to-read level (1–4) as well as a Guided Reading Level (A–P). Both of these systems will help you choose the right book for your child. Please refer to the back of each book for specific leveling information. Penguin Young Readers features esteemed authors and illustrators, stories about favorite characters, fascinating nonfiction, and more!

Happy Thanksgiving, Tiny!

LEVEL 1

GUIDED READING LEVEL **D**

This book is perfect for an **Emergent Reader** who:
• can read in a left-to-right and top-to-bottom progression;
• can recognize some beginning and ending letter sounds;
• can use picture clues to help tell the story; and
• can understand the basic plot and sequence of simple stories.

Here are some **activities** you can do during and after reading this book:
• Character Traits: One of Tiny's character traits is that he is clumsy. Write a list of some of his other traits.
• Make Connections: In this story, Tiny and Eliot are in a Thanksgiving play. Have you ever been part of a performance? Write a paragraph about the role you would want if you were in a play.

Remember, sharing the love of reading with a child is the best gift you can give!

—Sarah Fabiny, Editorial Director
Penguin Young Readers program

*Penguin Young Readers are leveled by independent reviewers applying the standards developed by Irene Fountas and Gay Su Pinnell in *Matching Books to Readers: Using Leveled Books in Guided Reading*, Heinemann, 1999.

For Benjamin—CM

To Roy Lessin, my brother in Christ. You have
invested so much in my life—I give thanks for
you! Phil. 2:13—RD

PENGUIN YOUNG READERS
An Imprint of Penguin Random House LLC

Text copyright © 2018 by Cari Meister. Illustrations copyright © 2018 by Richard D. Davis.
All rights reserved. Published by Penguin Young Readers, an imprint of Penguin Random House LLC,
345 Hudson Street, New York, New York 10014. Manufactured in China.

Library of Congress Cataloging-in-Publication Data is available.

ISBN 9781524783884 (pbk)   10 9 8 7 6 5 4 3 2 1
ISBN 9781524783891 (hc)   10 9 8 7 6 5 4 3 2

Happy Thanksgiving, TiNY!

by Cari Meister
illustrated by Rich Davis

Penguin Young Readers
An Imprint of Penguin Random House

Look, Tiny.

A Thanksgiving play!

4

6

I sing.

I dance.

7

I get a part.

I am an ear of corn.

8

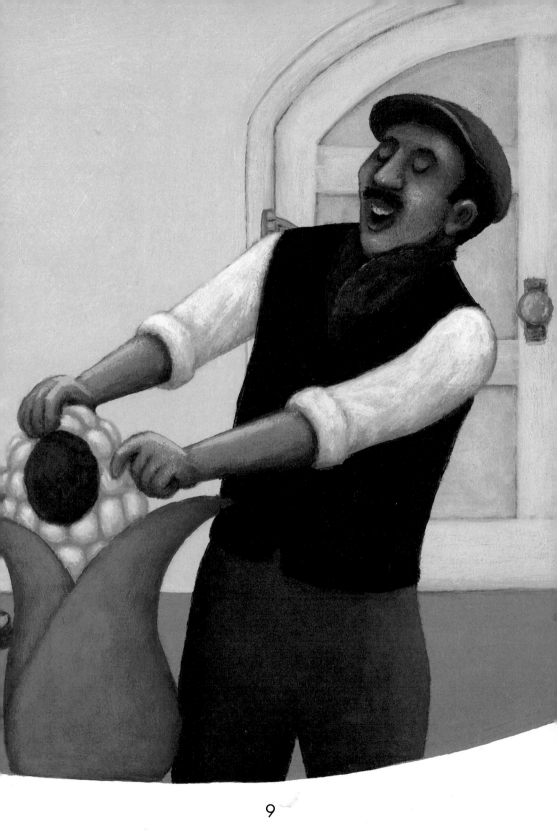

Tiny wants a part, too.

Sorry, Tiny.

There are no parts for dogs.

I know!

Tiny is big.

He can help.

Tiny helps with the set.

Oh no!

Stop, Tiny!

Tiny helps with the props.

Oh no!

Crash!

19

Sorry, Tiny.

You need to stay out.

I work on my lines.

Tiny waits.

Today is the show!

Oh no!

The turkey is sick.

Who will be the turkey?

Tiny will!

The play is fun.

Tiny is a good turkey.

Happy Thanksgiving, Tiny!